K.V. Twain

My Life with Salvador Dalí,

by Babou the Ocelot

Published by Cappas Press

Content © 2015 Diana Carligeanu (pen name: K.V. Twain)

Cover design © 2015 Diana Carligeanu, using a public domain photo of Salvador Dalí and pet ocelot Babou, taken by Roger Higgins on January 1, 1965, at New York's St. Regis Hotel. Photo repository: Library of Congress, Prints and Photographs Division, Washington, D.C. 20540-4730, U.S.A.

ISBN: 978-606939660-5

Contents

I

My name is Eli. Animals who live in the wild are given short and efficient names, which are easy to call in all contingencies. Ama, Pol, Rau, Sor, Tor, Zar. Names like those. My mamma named me Eli, and I carry my name with pride. Some say there's an Eli in the human kingdom too, but I am not concerned with such things. I asked mamma about the name of the land, and she said, "We can only name things which are ours, and the land isn't, we only inhabit it for a while, as long as we can." I asked mamma about her name too, and she said she's just mamma, and if I ever called her she would unfailingly hear. So mamma is mamma, and land is land.

Sometimes, when I perched up in a tree and looked over the land, eyes surveying carefully the territory to my left and right, a feeling of complete peace descended over me, like a whisper tapping my body and reaching through to my mind. I thought then that I would forever watch the land, that it was mine to watch, a most significant duty bestowed upon me by a wise and visionary predecessor. I felt certain that the fate of my race was vested in me, that I was its leader and protector, and I puffed out my chest to show that I welcomed the task and was well capable of fulfilling it.

A time came when I noticed a different land, one up above, at some distance, which was only visible once the day's light ceased. Then it glinted and sparkled. I wondered about it for a while and eventually asked mamma what it was. Her answer, which I trusted, was that the far-up land was not for us to reach or walk on, but to take comfort from and to use for guidance when hunting. The reason the far-up land sparkled was that there were little bright lights in it. I decided, in spite of my non-possession of them, to call them *schlundewassens.* There was also a large creature in that land, one whom I imagined guarding the lights as my mother guarded me, and that creature never moved but did somehow change shape from one moment to another. (Try as I might, I never caught her in the act of making herself over.) I was entirely captivated by her presence, by her alluring glowing body, and I named her *drom.* Both lands, the steady one right beneath my feet and the shimmery one way above my eyes, made a deep impression upon me.

I am a dreamer, which is to say that I have frequent dreams.

My first dream, which remained forever vivid in my mind, occurred during the day following the night of my first hunting lesson. That night my mother told me to follow her, as she would demonstrate the three stages of hunting: reconnoitering, pursuing, and pouncing. We stepped out of the den, mamma in front and I scudding behind her, feeling overjoyed at the prospect of a new experience. I growled a little, as best

I could, to show my happiness and my eagerness to observe and learn. The first stage, that of reconnoitering, consisted of stalking the land while sniffing the air for scents, as well as trying to spot any potential prey which might be lying about. The second stage, that of pursuing, meant deciding on a target and then making a stealthy advance for it, so as to ambush it when the right moment presented itself. The final stage, my favorite, was applying the swift winning maneuver of the pounce, claws extended and fangs biting into the prey. Mamma and I caught a rat and a rabbit that night, or rather mamma caught them while I observed the proceedings, and we returned to the den just as I was starting to feel slightly worn-out. I was extremely pleased, however, on account of being filled with the magnificent knowledge that I had graduated to a new level of understanding and of ocelotness itself. As I drifted off to sleep, I imagined launching myself upon a rabbit and claiming victory, and vowed with my remaining senses that I would become a skillful hunter and make mamma proud.

At some point during my slumber the dream came. Of course, only upon awakening and finding myself next to my mother did I realize that what had seemed all-too-real had not in fact been so. In this dream I was engaged in reconnoitering, that first stage of hunting, advancing with easy paces and focusing my eyes on my immediate surroundings. It soon became apparent that I could neither see any prey nor feel a single scent in the air—nothing reached my eyes or ears or whiskers,—all animals had vanished as far as I could sense. I became puzzled and alarmed, and decided to pause my ambling a while, so as to think over this terrible discovery. I brooded and fretted a long time, but found no way to tell what could possibly have caused all the animals to disappear. I wondered if mamma might know, but for some unaccountable reason I knew myself to be alone and unable to ask her. Presently I resumed my walkabout, hoping that the answer might eventually reveal itself. As I continued on, I noticed that the vegetation around me grew sparser and sparser, the shrubbery essential to my hunting rarer and rarer. I began to panic. I quickened my pace and before long I was running at nearly full speed, while all around me the barrenness and bleakness were growing. Very soon my nose picked up a scent, a fearsome foreign scent which I had not the ability to interpret. I again wanted to ask mamma for its meaning, but I was alone and so I kept running. Almost immediately, however, I found myself struggling to breathe, as waves of that dreadful scent wafted over and engulfed me. I now felt highly distressed, as I could see no escape from my ghastly predicament. At that very instant I awoke, which was a tremendous relief. I nuzzled up against my mother, rubbed my nose into her soft body, and tried to silently understand what I had just witnessed.

It was easy enough to comprehend the unreality of my wretched solitary adventures, but puzzling out the meaning of my dream—if there was one—struck me as a rather complicated affair. Hoping that I might someday get to the bottom of this dream and all the other dreams which might come, I resolved to henceforth count all of my dreams and memorize, to the best of my abilities, their subject matter.

During my time with mamma, in which I continued to learn to hunt and eventually hunted on my own, I counted a total of fourteen dreams. Some of the visions were good and others bad, which is to say that some I liked and others I didn't. My favorite ones were those in which I was rollicking about with my mother, and we playfully tackled each other. How I loved those, and how I loved the frolics! All my dreams were about life in the land, the day life and the night life: the hunting, exploring, playing, resting.

At one point I asked mamma whether she too had dreams, and whether hers were good and bad, like mine. She said, "Yes, that's how it is."

So you see, I was the only son of my mother, who was the only mother of me, and I was a dreamer, and so was she. We'd dream together, and awake together.

II

One grim day, sometime later, I awoke to a much colder reality. I was away from my mother, which I could tell the instant I called her and received no reply. I was also away from the land, away from the trees, shrubs, rabbits, deer—something that my eyes, ears, and whiskers all told me. I didn't know where I was and how I'd ended up there, but realized with mounting horror that it was a strange and unpleasant place, and some terrible misfortune had befallen me. My mind was dizzy with confusion and panic, and my body felt oppressed by a weakness I had only known in my very first dream. Before long I became aware of a vague nausea pervading my senses—a nausea which grew quickly into a distinct sensation of having had a foul meal, of having gorged on something akin to an old carcass. I felt sick to the very core of my being, and presently found myself involuntarily expunging the contents of my gut. This act caused the nausea to let up in some measure, if only a slight one. Still stupefied, I looked about me and noticed, a short distance away, another ocelot: a female, as judged by her scent, who looked no less confused than I was. For a moment I stared at her and she stared at me, and that's all either of us did. It then occurred to me that she must be either a friend or an enemy, and I should act accordingly. Before I did, however, she took the initiative to introduce herself: "I'm Mar," she said quietly. I then surmised that we were friends, or at least ocelots with no inimical intent toward each other. This made me feel, very briefly, a great surge of happiness within my being. I should probably have introduced myself at that point, told Mar my name, but I felt too overwhelmed by the swirl of thoughts in my head. I had noticed that Mar and I found ourselves in the midst of a vast assortment of hideous objects, things utterly foreign to me—and, by my guess, to Mar as well,—and I couldn't help thinking that we had to make an escape. I made an effort to think clearly and chase away the feebleness of my body, and soon signaled Mar to get going. I said my name was Eli while readying to move, and added that we had to get back to our dens.

Mar and I proceeded to run frantically about the new place, looking desperately for signs that could point us in the right direction. The more we ran, the more repulsed I felt by our surroundings. There were no signs to help us—there were only filthy objects and big grubby creatures standing in our way, thwarting our passage. As we ran and occasionally tried to clutch at this or that item, I became aware of the most disturbing fact yet: I no longer had claws or fangs! My eyes welled up with fury and sorrow, as the thought struck me that I was entirely done for. I kept running in bewilderment and misery, since there was nothing else to do, and eventually reached a place which resembled the land slightly more than the previous setting. There were trees here, and I rushed to mark one as mine and to clamber up: something I did with some difficulty, on account of my lack of claws. Mar sat herself in a tree close to mine, and it soon became apparent that she too was missing her claws and fangs. We fell still and tried to think, feeling forlorn and helpless.

While mulling over my situation and Mar's, it dawned on me that the recent misadventures might well be occurring in a mere dream, the fifteenth, which would doubtless reach a conclusion before long, leaving me ensconced safely in my den. The more I considered this possibility, the more probable it seemed, and I felt foolish for not sooner hitting upon this splendid explanation of events. After all, I had sufficient knowledge of dreams, having had fourteen of them. I smiled contentedly to myself, reasoning that all I had to do was await the consummation of the imaginary ordeal. I glanced over at Mar, silently anticipating her disappearance into thin air. Looking at her caused me to realize that she was pretty and that I didn't mind having her around for company, especially under the circumstances. Nevertheless, I felt confident that the dream would soon be over, and I preferred that outcome over the present one.

I continued to keep quiet and so did Mar, and after a time we dropped off into a snooze, and after another time we awoke. None of our circumstances was in any way altered, and I felt a great fright seizing my body.

Just then Mar spoke, saying that we clearly couldn't go back, that we were trapped and would have to cope as best we could. I wondered if she knew about dreams and further considered sharing my theory with her, but I ended up saying nothing: I merely mewed to indicate a sort of agreement, after which I sank deeper into despondency. I couldn't help contemplating the coming night and the impossibility of hunting in this new place, which afforded us—based on my observations up until then—neither prey nor enough shrubbery for cover; moreover, we were now wanting for claws and fangs, which played a crucial role in grabbing and biting. What a dismal dilemma Mar and I faced!

When night came, one of the grubby creatures brought out a repast for Mar and me. We could tell by the scent and by the way the creature pointed that it was food, and meant for us. It wasn't, however, food that Mar and I were used to having. There was no just-hunted, freshly-killed animal. We were hesitant to eat, and kept sniffing about the unfamiliar fare. (The creature thankfully left us in peace shortly after fetching the food, so we could do as we wished.) We began to eat when hunger told us to, but got little pleasure from doing so.

That night, a night without hunting, a night filled with deep worries and desperate questions, I sat up in my new tree and watched the drom and the schlundewassens. These, along with Mar, were my sole companions and singular source of comfort. I growled at them then for the first time, fervidly hoping for some sort of communication. I pricked up my ears, eager not to miss a forthcoming answer. I waited a while, then growled again and once more waited. There was no response, and the absence plunged me into bitter desolation. I began to think of the foul beings that had boldly burst into my life. Mar and I agreed that we hadn't seen their type before. They produced loud noises and gave off peculiar scents, all of which made for a rather insufferable appearance. I felt a strong desire to devour them, just so that I could rid myself of their offensiveness, but felt concerned about my lack of fangs and the possibility that doing away with the creatures might mean that Mar and I would subsequently become bereft of nourishment. (I didn't much care for the grub myself, it was more the fangs' absence that worried me, but I thought that Mar might want the beasts' food.) I considered asking Mar whether she too felt like eating the dreadful fiends, and whether we should put the idea into practice, but she appeared to be snoozing—perched again in a tree not far from mine,—and so I kept quiet. I then made an effort to recall the last time I had found myself in the land, with mamma, for I wished to understand what sort of incident was responsible for my sudden, terrible relocation. It seemed to me that mamma and I were playing close to our den, as was our habit, when a prodigious noise shocked my eardrums, causing me to rush confusedly into the den. Unfortunately, I was unable to recall any later happenings from the land: only a sense of intense dizziness and disorientation reached my still-disordered mind. I grew faint from the recollections, scant as they were, and consequently decided to focus my thoughts elsewhere. In fact, I endeavored to stop the train of thoughts altogether, to cease all reasoning and to enjoy the soundless beauty of the drom and the schlundewassens. I lifted up my gaze, and kept it aloft for a long time. At some point I could see, I fancied, a gentle shifting in the drom, a subtle stirring which resulted in greater fullness of face. A thrilling tingle then coursed through my body, and I fell into a deep, dark, dreamless slumber.

When I awoke, a stream of light seemingly playing on my face, Mar was alert and engaged in a penetrating examination of my being—a fact which made me feel somewhat embarrassed, for reasons I could not adequately fathom or articulate. None of the ugly beasts was around. I told Mar the names I had assigned, early in my life, to the pretty lights and the graceful creature in the far-up land, whom I had now come to regard as allies. Mar said that she too had given them names, names different from those I had conjured, but it didn't much matter what one called them: what mattered was that one should cherish them. I wondered then whether anyone besides Mar and me ever admired the drom and the schlundewassens, and felt half-sad and half-glad at the possibility that we might be the only animals to recognize and treasure, if silently, the beauty of those beings. Mar and I then turned our thoughts to our immediate circumstances. We determined that we would make an effort to learn all we could about the new surroundings, and wait—with as much patience as we could summon—to see how things progressed. It seemed a good idea, if we were ever to escape the hideous place we found ourselves in, to understand what it was all about. From then on I would apply myself diligently to the task of learning, and so would Mar.

The learning process began in next to no time, and proved a painful experience. It soon became apparent that the foul creatures—who called themselves people or humans, I slowly discovered—communicated in a language much different from that of ocelots. The loud noises I had perceived upon the first encounter, which had grated on and continued to vex my sensitive ears, were part of that language, if not the entire language. (They represented *words, palabras, paraules.*) It also became manifest that the people had not been informed of my name or Mar's, for they called out to us using the appellations *Babou* and *Bouba,* the former for myself and the latter for Mar. I find it impossible to describe to you my displeasure at this grave and needless disrespect. Speaking strictly for myself, not only did I have a name already, a beautiful one given to me by my mother, the only one entitled to give me a name, but I also found the designation *Babou* to be utterly unsuited to my being. *Babou* could well describe a fat round animal who relished the company of humans and might not object to being given a name by them, but it was most unbecoming to a fierce animal like me, whose life was—or was supposed to be—one of roaming the land. I protested wildly the first few times anyone called me Babou so as to show my annoyance, outright fury even, but I could not tell whether my message got through, on account of the language differences I have mentioned. Mar did not look kindly upon the new name business, either: she cringed, scowled, and grumbled. In view of our displeasure, we resolved never to accept the human designations, never to consider them ours, and to always remain Mar and Eli to ourselves.

Shortly after waking up in the new place I came across three gats, which is to say three animals who claimed to be gats and to reside in the area; they were somewhat smaller than ocelots, but otherwise similar in appearance and language. I was intrigued at first, as ocelots always are upon meeting beasts of a type never before encountered, but concluded soon enough that the new acquaintances weren't animals to eat, but rather animals to befriend. How thankful and relieved I felt at this discovery! The gats themselves were initially more startled than myself, arching their backs and warning me against taking further steps in their direction. So I stood a while, pitted as presumed adversary against the curious, searching, apprehensive eyes of the charming creatures before me. Then I pressed forward slowly, cautiously, calling out to say that I only desired to play. Some time passed in a game of advancement and retreat, which I imagined to be important and determining of the future relationship I might have with the creatures. A minor scuffle ensued when the gats judged that I had come too close to them, or trespassed on their territory, and the largest of them decided to strike a blow to my head; it was a firm blow, and I responded by swiftly rolling onto my back. We clarified things quickly after that, agreeing that friendliness rather than enmity was the way forward.

Once that decision was made, we proceeded with the introductions. The first gat, a young and shy gray male, was named Fiord. The second, a pure-black female who was slightly more grown and seemingly quite independent, was Aigua. The third, an elderly male with assorted stripes and a sad air, and the one with whom I had tussled, was Dos Pasos. All three gats lived on the streets and in various places which served them as shelter. They scavenged and begged for food, but they never had enough and as a result were quite thin. They explained that having a master was every gat's dream, since a master came with a home and a reliable supply of food. They asked whether I had a master, and I didn't know how to respond, but after further discussions and explanations of the term *master* I came to conclude that yes, I had a master now, perhaps even several. I deduced from this conversation that there was one key difference between gats and ocelots: gats wanted a master, while ocelots didn't. Even so, I liked the gats and was delighted to have discovered them. As soon as I arrived back at my new abode I told Mar about my remarkable finding. At the next meeting with the gats I introduced them to Mar, and vice versa. (It was on this occasion that I noticed, more acutely than before, Mar's diffident nature: while possessed of a pleasant disposition, she appeared to wish to make herself entirely inconspicuous.)

Meeting Fiord, Aigua, and Dos Pasos meant not only that Mar and I had additional and much appreciated company, but also that there was someone to whom we could put questions about people and their lives, by which we could make progress in our learning. And that we did.

The gats confirmed my impression that people were a peculiar sort of animal—peculiar, that is, on account of their strange habits and circumstances. For instance, they lived in elaborate homes and had an endless supply of food, which one never saw them hunting or begging for. (This caused the gats to speculate that humans were much like the small vexing creatures who burrowed into their furs and fed off of their bodies: it was just difficult to tell from whom people might be deriving their profit.) As far as the gats were able to tell, there were four broad categories of people, differing in appearance, sound, and scent: men, women, boys, and girls, with the last two of considerably smaller size than the others. (The gats guessed that the small ones were the offspring.) According to the gats, the offspring were charitable enough as a rule, but men and women were as likely to be cruel as kind, and one couldn't always fathom their nature at first sight. Therefore an animal like a gat or an ocelot had to carefully analyze each individual if he wished to get a sense of the specimen's temperament. The gats explained numerous other things, too many to count. They explained, for instance, the differences between indoors and outdoors, and between apartments and houses: information quite valuable in helping Mar and me make sense of our new environment.

Based on the conversations with the gats, Mar and I concluded that our new abode, which would no doubt prove temporary, was the place of one named Dalí, and that it was a house rather than an apartment. It wasn't very large, certainly not large enough for an ocelot— let alone two,—but it had a garden: the place where the trees called *olivos* stood, and where Mar and I spent much of our time.

All their knowledge the gats had acquired through the manifold interactions they'd had with humankind in the course of time. I hope you will allow me to recount some of their experiences in some detail, as I deem them important to a proper understanding of my new friends and possibly valuable in other ways. Aigua had always lived on the streets, or at least since as far back as her memory could reach. She had been nameless, at least to her knowledge, until Dos Pasos found her and named her. She longed for a proper home and someone who might dispel her many day-to-day problems, but felt keenly that she could not allow her yearnings to get in the way of her survival. Fiord had been in the care of a big and kindly man, in a house where multiple people lived, until he was given away to a man who lived in a different house and who put him out onto the carrers not much later. He tried to get back into both houses—they weren't too far off from each other, and Fiord tried now this and then that,—but he was always snubbed and rudely sent away. Abandoned by those he considered his masters, Fiord concluded that nothing should ever be offered someone without an earlier check that the object being offered is actually desired. Yet the most extraordinary story belonged to Dos Pasos, and I was so impressed by it that I would like to recount it in the self-same detail that my friend provided: it seems to me that nothing short of that particularity would do the story justice. Dos Pasos lived, from a young age, with a woman named Dolors—a small and delicate being, all vivacity concentrated in the sparkle of her eyes. She was good to him, which was evidenced by the fact that she provided him not only with the plain necessities required for a gat's subsistence, but also with frills which made for a more-than-decent, indeed quite sumptuous, living. Those frills included several resting places arranged specifically for Dos Pasos throughout the house; a number of enchanting toys for entertainment and diversion; a swarm of affectionate touches and kisses dispensed at all times; the right to sleep in Dolors' bed and to slip under her covers; and the most exquisite gift of all, dialogue, which was doubtless meant to benefit the gat in some way. (Dolors also took the trouble to find a name for her companion which would both befit him and hold a special meaning. Unfortunately, Dos Pasos could not recall the meaning of his appellation: he only remembered that he was named early on in his life, and Dolors explained the name to him on various occasions.) Dolors held numerous conversations with

Dos Pasos, on topics either trivial or significant, concerning the ways of humans and other beasts. The woman would read assorted papers and llibres and explain their substance to the gat, who would curl up on her knees or at her side and try to absorb the teachings. Remarkably, Dolors knew the importance of patience and repetition when trying to educate a gat: she would pronounce the same word or phrase multiple times while pointing to the object it described, and sometimes pronounce the same word or phrase on additional occasions, so that Dos Pasos would learn to make associations. And how he loved to learn! (A thirst for learning remained with this gat for the rest of his life.) Dos Pasos' favorite expression, of all he had been taught, was *faire le clown*; he described this as something that most humans do now and then, and some do at all times: they pretend to be silly, not realizing that they are silly already. Dolors never took Dos Pasos on trips, as Dalí did with Mar and me, but my friend was perfectly happy to roam the garden by his house and to otherwise stay indoors. So they lived together, woman and gat in faultless harmony, until the day when Dos Pasos found Dolors lying motionless in her llit and refusing to wake. First Dos Pasos surmised that she was trying to engage him in a game, after all they played games often enough, but then he pressed his paw gently onto her face and realized that she was colder than she'd ever been before, and something must be amiss. He tried all the habitual methods of rousing Dolors—tugging at the bed-covers; tapping her left cheek, right cheek, and nose; biting the nose—before resorting to more unusual techniques, such as doing small repetitive jumps on top of the woman's body. At any moment he expected a hand to come up and ward him off, or a grumpy voice to rebuke him, but neither came. Dos Pasos meowed protestingly, then whimpered feebly. Dolors wouldn't be awakened. Two lonely days and nights passed before someone came to the house: it was a woman who threw Dos Pasos out onto the carrers without making the slightest attempt to speak to him. That's how my friend became an alley gat, with a life given by his mother and an identity given by a wise woman who bothered to raise and educate him. Dos Pasos kept the same whereabouts as before and visited Dolors' house multiple times, which is to say that he remained on the outside of it, peering into its windows. Yet he never saw Dolors again. The house was empty for a time, then occupied by a pair who had no interest in gats, judging from the fact that they shooed Dos Pasos away the first time they saw him pad about the place.

One day, while ambling about with the gats, my eye was caught by another animal standing at a distance. He was feasting on the ground's covering, and calmly flicking his tail. His body, mostly dark-colored but light in places, was larger and sturdier than that of gats or ocelots, and his four limbs were longer and stiffer. The look of him bore, I thought, a slight resemblance to that of a deer—a majestic beast residing in the land of my mother. Feeling quite struck with awe and pleasure at this unusual appearance, I let out a chuckle and asked Dos Pasos about the creature's identity. Dos

Pasos explained that this was a *ruc*, an object of admiration for those who have good knowledge of the animal world and at once the hero of many stories—albeit one often overlooked. Dolors had harbored a special fondness for rucs, one nearly rivaling that felt for gats, and had repeatedly shown Dos Pasos pictures of a girl in the company of this thrilling specimen. I stared at the animal for a long time, trying to take in all the details of his handsome body, and wondered what other charming creatures I might encounter in this place.

The chief hero in stories, according to Dos Pasos, was *Mala Sort*, unless this was the name of an important character or gat whom Dolors had known before him—one even more important than the ruc. It was with great frequency that Dolors had spoken of Mala Sort, which was why Dos Pasos had made this guess.

I came across a great many beasts in my new life, right from the beginning and to the very end of my recollections, but the vast majority of them were humans and they were nowhere near as enchanting as the ruc. Indeed, the nearly-constant swarm of people was one of the things that bothered me most in this second existence. Four of the people became a permanent feature in my life, while the others came and went and sometimes returned. The four were named Dalí, Gala, Peter, and Isidor—something that Mar and I worked out in time, since these animals, unlike the gats, did not introduce themselves to us.

Dalí was the most striking of all and initially I looked to him somewhat fondly, for he had whiskers and I thought that made him a special creature, different from the other people, one who must be kind to ocelots if not somehow related. As time passed I grew more and more disillusioned with Dalí, for reasons I shall endeavor to make clear. Gala, the only woman among the people I have mentioned, had other names in addition to Gala. They included Galushka, Gradiva, Oliva, Oliveta, and Lionette. Mar and I reached this conclusion after seeing Dalí call out to Gala using all those different names and receiving a response every single time. As you can perhaps imagine, this was quite a baffling discovery. Never before had Mar or I encountered such a multi-named animal! Fiord, Aigua, and Dos Pasos, whose opinions we sought in this matter, were agreed that none of them had seen anyone with more than a name. We thus deduced that Gala must be an exceptional case, and until other such beings showed up she'd be The Creature Of Many Names. Peter was an unremarkable beast, like most of those who came and went. He didn't inspire feelings of any kind in me, except when he did things I disliked, or forced me to do things I disliked. At such times I felt a positive loathing for him, and often hissed to show my displeasure. Peter was a frequent presence at Dalí's house, and came on many of the trips which Mar and I were forced to undertake. Isidor was a quiet, unassuming fellow who lived close to Dalí's place and spent most of his time indoors. In time we managed to steal a glance into his home, and determined that his pastimes were much like Dalí's.

A brief while into my new existence, I found myself facing a *mirall*. (It was later that Dos Pasos told me the name of the unusual item.) Straightaway I thought that I had before me another ocelot, a third one who had presumably been brought to keep Mar and me company. I rushed toward him, then immediately drew back—realizing that he might have felt as distraught as Mar and I had felt upon our arrival. I kept looking at him, trying to think up suitable ways to approach, and soon it dawned on me that no scent issued from the creature, and moreover he was moving in the exact same way that I was, making the very same gestures: if I turned, he turned; if I hesitated, he too hesitated. These traits were undoubtedly peculiar, and they greatly incited my curiosity. I took a leap in the creature's direction, not being able to control my excitement, and felt my body hit a hard surface which was decidedly not an ocelot. This collision came as a terrible shock: the creature before my eyes wore the same stunned look which I imagined myself to be wearing. Presently I was struck by the astounding recognition that we were one and the same, the creature and I, that I was merely watching my own body. I consequently lost all interest in the strange object—quite revolting I found it!—despite the fact that it revealed me to be as fine-looking as I had always known myself to be. I learned gradually, however, that many humans were fond of spending time in front of the mirall, twisting and twirling and giggling while commenting on I don't know what. On numerous occasions I saw Dalí and Gala cast appreciative glances in its direction, apparently delighted at the apparition before their eyes.

Around the same time as the mirall incident, I had my fifteenth dream. It was a bad one. Here is what happened: I was in the land; I had been chasing a rat for some distance and was now making my way into its den; as I was entering, the den before me turned into a filthy place akin to the one I was now inhabiting in real life, and the rat became one of the people. At that point I turned around and ran as fast as I could, but as I was thus racing I became aware that I myself was gradually turning into a rat, my magnificent stature soon reduced to a lowly presence. I reached and entered my own den, or what I believed to be my den, but there I was faced with a family of rats. I opened my mouth to protest, to say, "Please excuse me, this is a serious mistake, I myself am an ocelot and have no business being here, this isn't my home, it must be yours, really you can have it, I'm going now," but only a pitiful squeak came out. That's when the dream ended. I sighed and tried to put it out of my mind, despite having once resolved to memorize the contents of my dreams. I again considered asking Mar whether she too had dreams, and telling her about my own. This time, after mulling the matter a while and concluding that chatting about dreams might be a nice diversion, I did make an inquiry. To my great disappointment, Mar replied that she herself had no dreams. She said so rather curtly, and I was taken aback. I decided then to keep my dreams to myself, and share them with mamma when I got back to her. I had to get back to her someday.

After our awkward introduction and the shock of our new reality, Mar and I settled quickly into an easy camaraderie in which the proper balance of closeness and distance was typically maintained and only rarely disturbed. We knew each other to be unhappy and facing the same predicament, something which needed no articulating, and we tried not to further aggravate our plight; instead, we kept to an unspoken imperative of being good friends and allies. We devised several games to pass the time when bored and in the mood for fun, occasionally inviting the gats to join us. We played three main games—besides the basic one of tussling, in which Mar and I took turns asserting our power,—only two of which were competitive. The first game was the fairly simple one of splashing about in puddles which formed on the ground after pluges; the second was the find-me game, which was taught to us by Dos Pasos and entailed locating a hideout which then had to be discovered by the other game participants; and the third was the chasing and catching of birds and butterflies. It was this last game that we generally involved the gats in; they were as adept as Mar and me at catching birds, but butterflies eluded us all most of the time, and as a result we contented ourselves with admiring their tantalizing flights from a distance. (There were butterflies in Dalí's house too, but they never moved, they remained always in one place, static and smooth, no thrill emanating from their small stilted bodies.)

One of my first discoveries about people, one made in relation to their love for the mirall, was that they were not what they appeared to be: they had many different skins, of different textures and colors and smells, multiple skins for the day and multiple skins for the night, which were changed with astonishing frequency. It was when making such changes that people were most likely to twirl before the mirall and take pleasure in their appearance. That finding fascinated me, for ocelots and all the other animals I knew had only one skin, and it was inconceivable that one should shed it, let alone replace it periodically with other skins. Mitjons were some of the pieces of skin that people put on, along with other pieces. Here is how I learned this: A time came when I started to miss hunting terribly. There seemed to be nothing I could pounce on without receiving blows to my head or other parts of my body, except for things I found outside—which were far from satisfying and not always available, as I often found myself stuck indoors. Before long, however, I did stumble upon something inside that I could launch attacks upon, play with, and nibble at: some small soft objects lying about in one of Dalí's rooms. What started as a natural, harmless attempt to distract myself from boredom and from the pain of being unable to hunt soon became one of my favorite ways to pass the time. I only learned what the objects were when I saw Dalí looking for them and, upon finding them, carefully attach them to his body. (The name, *mitjons*, I got from Dos Pasos.) Dalí didn't seem to mind my habit of playing with those items, judging from the fact that he showed little displeasure upon catching me in the act. I therefore kept on with my pastime, although I tried to engage in it when Dalí wasn't around to see me. I'd wait for him to disappear, locate the mitjons, and pounce!

Dalí spent significant amounts of time in the forbidden room, this being a space in Dalí's house which Mar and I were kept away from. Dalí was usually there by himself, and as the days passed I grew increasingly curious as to the nature of his activities. At times I could make out a continuous low hum coming from within the room's bounds, and then my curiosity heightened. Mar and I peeked into the room a few times, as we did with Isidor's place, and concluded that Dalí was engaged in some form of image-making. A very peculiar occupation this was, one with no obvious benefit to anybody, but I guessed that this may have been mere play for Dalí, in the same way that nibbling on his mitjons was for me. Mar and I informed the gats about Dalí's image-making at the first opportunity we got, and they were incredulous and said they'd never seen anything like it. I invited them to come near Dalí's house on some days, in case the people were out or I found a way to let the gats into the forbidden room, but upon seeing the house Dos Pasos remarked that it was one to be avoided, one inimical to gats. I demanded elucidation, but Dos Pasos merely said that my master was not a friend of gats, and gats were not friends of his.

Dream no. 16: I found myself observing the goings-on inside a room where all manner of animals, gats and ocelots and rabbits and others, were being flung about the place and kicked against various objects, by Dalí and two other people who were unknown to me. The beasts were whimpering and groaning, while their tormentors were cackling hideously and delighting in the spectacle. In a short while, however, the wretched animals were gone and it was the three people who were being hurled about, by a great unseen force which wiped out their glee and gave them grief instead. The people were now gnashing their teeth in fury and frustration, for they felt entirely hopeless and doomed. (I observed their feelings in addition to their actions.) The dream ended just as I was beginning to wonder about the nature of the force responsible for the swift reversal of the people's fortunes.

Another early observation of mine, this one still more startling, was that noises were produced not only by people's mouths, but also by a contraption found inside Dalí's house. "Escuchemos música!" Dalí would cry excitedly, and he would touch the contraption and prodigious sounds would hurl themselves, in big waves, upon my delicate ears. The first time I witnessed this phenomenon I became quite scared, as I did not understand the meaning of the reverberations, and to my mind there was something utterly frightening about a machine which generated jingles and jangles and whistles. On occasion people's voices themselves seemed to come out of the device, like big menacing creatures leaping upon me, and then I became even more alarmed. I hoped that Dalí would someday explain these happenings to Mar and me, but he never did. Fiord and Aigua were entirely unable to elucidate the matter; only Dos Pasos had any knowledge of it, and all he could say was that the sounds were sometimes *música* and other times people's voices. Not long afterward I came to understand what música was and to consider it much more enjoyable than people's speech. Oftentimes it lulled me into a sense of peace and calm, which made me feel as though I had been transported back into the land. As for the wondrous sound-making machine, none of the gats knew its name, and therefore Mar and I termed it simply *sound machine*.

I wondered whether the numerous objects surrounding people were essential to their survival, or else mere accessories of questionable merit—like Mar and myself. Noticing that people did not actually use many of those objects, I could not help but conclude that the latter was true. It would have been nice to know whether the objects, ever-present and haphazardly arranged, often standing in my path and Mar's, were all owned and named by people, but this was a difficult question to which not even Dos Pasos had a definitive answer.

While many things intrigued me in my new life, llibres held a special appeal. I gathered, listening to Dos Pasos' account of his life with Dolors, that llibres were an instrument of learning, a means of gaining knowledge about the world. If one studied assiduously and reached a high level of knowledge—how high I wouldn't be able to say,—one might be admitted into the ranks of those named *culto, refinado, cultivé*, which everyone agreed was a terrific honor. All this was true for people, but seeing Dos Pasos in action, watching him gain the respect of his friends for the knowledge and wisdom he displayed, I concluded that it applied equally to beasts like us. I tried to envision the attention I could command if I added great cleverness to my striking looks, the name I could make for myself if I combined mental sophistication with physical loveliness. Perhaps I could earn the respect of both humans and non-humans, perhaps they would come to say, "There goes Eli, the ocelot who, through sheer willpower and tenacity, has become culto and distinguished." My name might then be carried across many lands, and my mother might hear of me and my good reputation even if I did not physically reach her. How proud she would be! How marvelous this would be! Unfortunately, the realization soon struck me that no matter how much fame I might win among ocelots or gats, I would never be celebrated by humans, for the differences in our languages would prevent them from guessing the extent of my cleverness. This new thought dampened my enthusiasm to some extent, but did not erase my desire to become cultivé. I wanted to become as learned as Dos Pasos and Dolors!

Numerous times I expressed to Dalí my desire to be educated, and urged him to read and explain things to me, but nearly all of my efforts proved fruitless. In fact, it was much more common for Gala to read to Dalí than for Dalí to read to me or Mar. This activity occurred not as the first thing in the day, but as a later pastime, after Dalí had spent a while hidden away in various rooms or else going out for strolls. I wasn't generally stopped from attending these reading sessions, but on a good number of occasions I chose to slink away and take a nap or else sit up in a tree, engrossed in deep reverie. You might think that such behavior, no doubt slothful in appearance, stood in direct contradiction to my desire to become educated, and was nothing but solid proof that I wasn't ready to apply myself to the toil of learning. Should you be thus inclined to think, I urge you to take account of these two facts: first, Gala read for Dalí's pleasure, rather than mine, and no thought was given to the fact that I, an unlearned animal, badly wanted to understand what was being said, and needed some explanations in order to do so; secondly, unlike Dos Pasos, a gat who was content to spend much of his time indoors, I quickly developed an ache for the world outside, and found myself fidgeting and wishing to get away from the closed space in which the reading sessions were typically held.

Dream no. 17: I, an ocelot, was having a conversation with Dalí. We were outside, and it was night. I could understand Dalí's words perfectly well, but was uncertain whether he could understand mine. Dalí was fixing me with big black-and-white eyes, nearly giving me a fright, and saying, "You have to reach for the stars, Babou, that's why they are there; one has to reach for them, and touch them!" As he pointed to the far-up land I realized that he was talking about the schlundewassens. Remembering what my mother had told me about that land, because I still had the memory of that lesson, I grew agitated and started to protest. I said, "No! You don't understand! The schlundewassens are not there to be reached; they are there to guide us and to give us comfort, that's all. And my name is not Babou! You are a fool! A fool!" As Dalí kept on watching me with much the same expression as before, now only slightly more amused, I began to doubt that he could understand me. This thought made me severely despondent.

The word *vamonos* marked the beginning of a trip, which could take a little while or a much longer time, which I could not even keep track of. Mar and I were never consulted about the destination, so we never knew, when setting out, where we would end up. (Even supposing that someone had managed to solicit our opinion in a language that we could understand, we would have had to make a reply which the other party could in turn comprehend: a likely impossible task.) Dalí seemed happiest when he said, "Vamos a la playa!" which he did before we headed out for the playa. Sometimes he even added, "Beach, Babou, we're going to the beach!" which made me think that perhaps he was trying to educate me about the meaning of words—something I was always learning. I understood after the first such trip that the playa was the place near the big pool of water, which I had previously seen from a distance. Every time we reached this particular destination Dalí went into a frenzy of excitement. He would pace up and down and exclaim, then do some more pacing and exclaiming. I myself did not understand what the fuss was about, for the playa did not possess the usual features that delight an ocelot. Moreover, I was unable to roam to my satisfaction on account of having a loathsome contraption fitted around my neck, and being pushed and pulled constantly through the use of another contraption, connected to the first one. Those nasty devices accompanied me on most trips, and I soon came to detest all outings which involved them. No matter how strenuously I tried to dodge, there was no escaping, for there was nowhere to turn once one of the people had caught hold of me. I asked the gats whether they had ever endured such tortures as I had to suffer at the playa and on other excursions. They said they hadn't, and explained that the contraptions which I described were *collaret* and *corretja*, respectively, and they were routinely forced on dogs— dogs being animals who, like gats, had a master if they were lucky and didn't have one if they weren't. Indeed, dogs were the only animals whom the gats had seen wearing collarets and corretges. I hadn't seen dogs up until then, and the information that other animals wore those pesky contrivances calmed my natural revulsion to some extent.

The name for Dalí's whiskers was *moustache*. Other people had moustaches, too—although they were significantly different from Dalí's, not resembling the whiskers of gats or ocelots. Peter himself had a moustache. I found it extraordinary that the same name could apply to things which were dissimilar, and I much wanted for someone to explain to me why this was so. Unfortunately, the gats were ignorant on this matter and the humans around me rarely understood or answered my questions.

The wonderlands occupied much of Dalí's time and energy, now and then giving rise to a positive frenzy of activity and emotion. The wonderland having to do with Perpignan prompted one such period of excitement: Dalí spent considerable amounts of time speaking of *gare* and *perpignan,* as well as the *centre de l'univers.* On and on he'd prattle, twirling his moustache, until I became thoroughly bored— notwithstanding my curiosity about the meaning of *perpignan,*—and decided to stop paying attention. Eventually a day came when I noticed the image had grown to an extraordinary size, and then another day came when I saw Dalí, wildly flinging his limbs about and speaking feverishly of the *centre de l'univers,* apparently explain various things to a group of visitors. Those same guests ended up taking the image away, removing it from Dalí's place, an act which rendered me speechless: how was it that Dalí could labor so intensely, so passionately, on the creation of an object and then place the object, with no obvious fight, into the hands of others? Not only this, but once the creatures had gone Dalí looked positively thrilled, like an ocelot made happy by a pleasant nap or a productive hunt, carrying a broad smile on his face. (This was the face which Dalí typically displayed upon emerging from the forbidden room, after a period spent toiling away.) This made no sense! I caught on straightaway and even growled at Dalí, once I'd regained my powers of speech, that it made no sense! Had I been told then, in no uncertain terms, to go after the evil beasts who seized Dalí's wonderland, I would have rushed to do so. But alas, no such command came. Dalí's face was one of utter contentment, causing me both bewilderment and embarrassment for my judgment. I never found resolution to that particular riddle, which was repeated on a number of occasions, but luckily I did come to learn the meaning of *perpignan*: this was nothing other than the place where Dalí, Gala, Peter, Mar, and I stepped onto the machine running over ground, in order to arrive somewhere else. That trip was repeated quite a large number of times, which is why I can remember its details with some precision and also why I concluded that Dalí and Gala must have derived some pleasure from it. On approaching that place of departure, Dalí would cry, "Perpignan!" as excitedly as he cried, "Vamos a la playa!" As for the *centre de l'univers,* I couldn't tell you what it was, or whether it had any importance.

In time I began to watch for those words, like *vamonos*, which signaled that an outing was being prepared. I detected the following: *journey, trip, excursion, excursión, salida, viatge,* and *voyage. Trip, excursion, excursión,* and *salida* worried me less than the others, as they generally announced brief outings rather than prolonged affairs, which were always more troublesome. Still, since even quick jaunts typically involved the collaret and the corretja, I became agitated just the same. And so, regardless of the sort of outing that was in the offing, I tried to melt away into some corner of the house or else into a shrub outside, so as to evade capture. Nevertheless, my stratagem was complicated by the fact that any amount of time could pass between the mention of one of those words and my capture for the purpose of attaching the loathed contraptions to my body. It was right after that attachment that the word *vamonos* would come, and we would go out. You see, I could go into hiding for a while, but not for an exceedingly long time—not least because I'd get hungry, and have to come out to eat. Mar was, naturally enough, facing the same dilemma. We therefore decided to seek other clues as to the timing of outings. Analyzing the actions of people and of Dalí in particular, we determined that at some point between the utterance of the first trip-indicating word and the articulation of the final one, *vamonos*, usually closer to the latter, Dalí—and sometimes other people, if they were around—made a change of skins. The skin that Dalí changed into was always as hideous as the one he'd just discarded, if not more so, which prompted Mar and me to wonder why Dalí ever bothered with that transformation. We never understood the meaning of his act, yet were glad to have one more pointer which could help us plan our escape. We now knew that we had to disappear shortly before, during, or right after the skin-change. It was safer to do so beforehand, as not much time was left afterward. However, it was extremely difficult to tell when a skin-change was coming, and whether it was coming because an outing was imminent. As I have explained, the skin changes were a frequent event, occurring every morning and every night, and throughout the day too—sometimes shortly before Dalí received visitors. To make matters worse, as nocturnal beasts Mar and I had to take naps during the day, when the people were active, and thus weren't always able to monitor comings and goings, let alone subtle gestures which might foretell small or big changes in our lives. Even if Mar and I took our snoozes in turns, the one who remained awake could easily lapse in one's alertness on account of getting tired or bored or distracted by assorted activities of the mind and the body. Due to all these intricacies, Mar and I only rarely managed to evade capture prior to an excursion. In fact, I can recall no more than five occasions when we were entirely successful; all of those times we were aided by the fact that we were outside, and slipped into shrubs before anyone could catch us. Many times we were only partially successful, with one of us escaping and the other being caught and dragged on some trip or another. On those occasions the one left behind had a nice enough time, I mean nice enough when considering the circumstances, while the one going forth generally ended up wretched, as a result of the trying nature of trips and the absence of ocelot companionship. I didn't like going on trips by myself, with only people for company; I didn't like not going on trips when it meant that Mar had to go, because then I worried for her and missed her presence; and I didn't like going on trips with Mar because that meant we were both unhappier than usual, even if together.

Long trips typically involved being transported in a machine running on land, on water, or high up in the air. The first two kinds of machines were large and frightening, with many people in them, a real pain altogether. I especially disliked being carried over water, as that always made me particularly nervous and sick to my stomach. The water trips lasted a long time too, or so it seemed, causing me to wonder whether I would ever again see trees and birds and butterflies. The only pleasurable activities during those trips were spending time with Mar, who was usually brought along; watching the drom and the schlundewassens at night; and thinking of the tales I'd be able to relate to the gats when—or if—we were reunited. The place we eventually arrived at was always an apartment, with no garden around but many people coming and going, a real disappointment altogether. I was often confined indoors, with little space to roam, no trees to climb, and no far-up land to admire at night. Even Dalí's mitjons could not provide enough diversion at such times, as I inevitably became exceptionally bored.

One time, during one of the voyages upon ground, my attention was drawn to a large and frantic flock of birds who gave me the impression that those creatures themselves were undertaking a voyage, or perhaps preparing for one. In times past I might have wanted to chase and catch them, but now I merely wanted to watch them and delight in their fantastical movements. Fast-fleeing flashes of wonder they seemed, flapping their wings in this world or in other worlds. Unfortunately, I was nearly blinded by light and had to close my eyes, which prevented me from properly observing the birds' flight. I wanted to call out to them, to say I know not what, but at the same time I felt that the exercise would be utterly pointless. I kept forcing open my eyes and striving to see, at times craning my neck and pulling on my corretja, until the birds faded away into the distance.

As a consequence of the pronounced and prolonged tedium I endured when forced indoors, I often wound up passing the time simply pondering various aspects of my life and the people's life. In such moments I found myself thinking, time and again, that Dalí could make a fine beast, if only some adjustments were made to his body and behavior. If Dalí were to speak less and more softly—walk and climb using all four limbs—acquire fangs and claws, plus a decent skin with nice fur—hunt instead of playing or laboring on his wonderlands, then he'd be a much improved being! The more I contemplated this scenario, the more it excited me. How I wished that I'd had the power to make Dalí into a lovely animal! Then we could speak the same language, perhaps even become friends and share stories... As things stood, however, I had no such power and felt doomed to a life of silent agony in the company of creatures who didn't understand me. It struck me as a disgrace that people should be allowed to change ocelots, but ocelots should not be allowed to change people. I shared that thought with Mar one day, "Wouldn't it be wonderful to have the power to change people?" and she agreed. Later on I solicited the gats' opinion, and also inquired whether they'd ever changed people. They answered, quietly and sadly, that as far as they could tell it was always people who did the changing: gats, dogs, and ocelots had to simply resign themselves to whatever life sent their way. I thought that such a shameful state of affairs could not continue much longer, and someone should take it upon themselves to remedy the matter. But what could possibly be done, and what could be done specifically by us gats and ocelots? *Vouloir, c'est pouvoir,* I heard people say, and I worked out the meaning of those words, but they were clearly not right: having the desire to change things was not enough to actually change them. Even if Mar and I managed to overpower the people, making them into creatures like us seemed a hopeless task.

I also wondered, in the course of my ruminations, what sort of direction things might have taken if Mar and I had met under different circumstances. Had we met in the land where I lived, in an all-too-brief phase of my life, with my mother, perhaps we would have given in to some kind of love; or perhaps I would have been rejected in favor of another ocelot, one deemed more appealing or suitable. "Who's to say?" I thought. It seemed to me that one could never tell how things would have unfolded in an alternate reality, one that was never lived and existed only as an image in one's mind; one could venture guesses, build theories, make predictions, and ultimately hope—a natural enough inclination, you will doubtless agree—that all happenings would have been exactly as desired. But then it was possible for the sought-after results to fail to materialize even with the preferred conditions in place. That, I have to say, appeared to me at least as profound a letdown as the deplorable state of affairs in which one is deprived of the right kind of environment. In the latter case one can still hold onto hope—which some might judge a mere illusion, but which is a helpful feeling nonetheless,—while in the former scenario all hope, or illusion, is wiped out. This consideration made me realize that it's terribly difficult to know what to wish for, as every situation holds its own troubles and risks. And it is, for the same reason, equally difficult to know whether one has been blessed or accursed, or both. It could well be, I went on thinking, that my own situation was not as dire as I generally reckoned it to be, or that all feasible alternatives would have been equally dire if explored, involving the same mixture of pain and pleasure, if not a more displeasing blend. Someone did say, after all, *Il faut laisser aller le monde comme il va,* by which I believe he meant that one must let things be what they are. This last thought soothed my spirit to some degree, though I continued to yearn for a different outcome for Mar and myself.

The place we reached after getting on the horrid machine departing from Perpignan was always the same: a large noisy crowded locale where Dalí and his human companions, along with Mar and myself, lived in an apartment—one which, like Dalí's house, was not spacious enough to properly accommodate two ocelots. (There is a certain amount of exercise which an ocelot must take if he is to feel healthy and content, and this was not possible in the circumstances.) All sorts of curious objects adorned this apartment, making life within its confines an even more arduous task for Mar and me. Trees there were in the vicinity, but we had no occasion to get to them apart from the times when Dalí or Peter took us there—something which happened all too seldom for my liking and Mar's. Feeling disoriented and discontent, controlled and curtailed, Mar and I spent much of our time sat in the spaces which allowed us, from inside the apartment, to look upon the trees outside. On several occasions Dalí pointed in the direction we were looking and called out, "Jardin des tuileries!" which I assumed to be a reference to that place of trees.

Looking out on the trees, I sometimes wondered how many ocelots might be in how many apartments, with lives separate from their destinies, and why Mar and I never saw them. I also wondered whether people ever ended up wrenched from their fates, stuck in lives which weren't truly theirs. Still, it seemed to me that the chief puzzle of my new life, the mystery sitting atop all other mysteries, was why the people had brought Mar and me to live with them. It was easy to see that we did not belong together, different as we were in our characters and habits and tastes. Moreover, there was no real interest in us—as evidenced by the fact that no one ever spent much time educating Mar and me,—and we ocelots weren't asked to perform any particular function, apart from accompanying the people on trips. So why? Why were we ever separated from our land and our mothers, carried into this chaos and confusion, this jumble and disarray? I could only assume, in the absence of anyone shedding light on the matter, that Mar and I were enduring punishment for some terrible deed we had committed and forgotten about. I tried to think what that deed might have been in my case, but nothing came to mind. This important, non-answerable riddle ate away at me, sinking my spirits ever lower. I missed the freedom to roam; I missed the simplicity of my life with mamma; I missed the deep quiet of the land, punctured only by the occasional cries of birds, the calls of monkeys, and the hissing of snakes. Increasingly I found myself having a desire to perish, to jump out of my life, even if right into the jaws of a more formidable animal, to perish like the rabbit or the rat.

When I wasn't confined indoors, I was taken outside for strolls, with Dalí and sometimes Gala and Peter too. (Mar was often taken along as well, to my sorrow and gladness.) We often entered enclosures whose name seemed to be one of *store* or *boutique* or *tienda*—based on the conversations which Dalí carried on with others. These enclosures were agglomerations of people and objects and noises, and were highly stifling and irritating to me, even more so than Dalí's house or the apartments I was made to live in. Many times I felt barely able to breathe, and at such times I became very agitated and tried to signal through my growls that I had to get out. To my profound disappointment and distress, Dalí and his companions rarely understood what I sought to communicate. As such, it was uncommon for me to get my wish for freedom, even the limited freedom of roaming about on a corretja, fulfilled. Dalí repeatedly started conversations with other people inside these enclosures, and sometimes other people started conversations with him. Indeed, talking was the main activity going on around me. Everyone talked and talked and talked, their tongues running faster and longer than ocelots' jaws at eating time! Sometimes people even spoke about Mar and me, which I could tell from their mention of Bouba and Babou, but what they actually said lay beyond my comprehension abilities. Some of those speaking with Dalí, people whom I hadn't previously seen, approached to stroke my fur and say I know not what to me or about me. I didn't like their attention, and wanted them to go away. (Indeed, I couldn't describe to you how repulsed I felt by the touch of humans. The mere sight of their greedy, grasping hands making for my figure made me tetchy and desperate for escape, and often I snarled and jerked my body so as to evade the looming rub. But alas, there was nowhere to go, caught firmly as I was by the corretja or in the hold of someone like Peter.) However, it occurred to me that certain of these people might perhaps understand my language—despite the clear failure of Dalí and his regular companions to do so,—and consequently I tried to tell them of my suffering. I explained very clearly, to a good number of them, that I did not belong with the people and had to get back to the land. Whenever a new person came to converse with Dalí, fresh hope arose in me that this time it might be different, this time I might get through. Yet despite my considerable efforts no one ever gave any sign of understanding my condition or wanting to answer my plea, and after a while I gave up.

At times, often just as I tried to slink off to sleep, my mind felt so jumbled and shaky that I had the distinct sensation of words dancing within it, as though caught in a great mocking whirl. *Soirée... fait accompli... mise en abyme...* woo! woo! *divertissement... meissonier... las meninas...* woo! woo!... *velázquez... réaliste... surréaliste...* woo! woo! *verde... deseo... alma...* Swiveling, sneering, twirling, tittering, the un-comprehended sounds of people delighted in my helplessness.

Dream no. 28: I was speaking to a strange human, one with the stature of a boy and the scent of a man, while weighing him up and wondering what to make of him. I felt glad that he couldn't access my thoughts, for I believed that he would have been peeved to know them. But then he too seemed to be sizing me up, wondering about my type. I told him what in real life I had told many: that the world of people was alien to me, that I did not share its characteristics and customs, and that my spirit yearned to get away from it and return to the land of my mother. To my considerable surprise, the strange man-boy said that he too was an outsider in the world of people, despite being human himself. He said, "We are all visitors, desired or not, and some of us don't even want to be visiting." I couldn't quite decipher the meaning of that speech, but it looked as though we were essentially in agreement, so we made plans to escape together. I informed him that I could not leave without Mar, and asked him to wait for me to bring her. I went off searching for Mar, and after a while I found her; but the curious boy-man vanished in the intervening time, and was subsequently nowhere to be found. Mar and I couldn't make our escape without him, and therefore remained entrapped in our lamentable lives.

Once, while out on a stroll with Dalí and Peter, I came upon dogs—those creatures of whom the gats had spoken,—who struck me as small and rash, and made my anger increase a thousandfold. How could anyone treat an ocelot like a dog, how could anyone think that an ocelot belonged on a corretja! Clearly, the people were entirely ignorant about the nature of ocelots, or else awfully cruel to inflict such treatment on us. It was shortly after that upsetting vision that I had my thirty-third dream: I was roaming about a strange place, searching for prey but failing to see any, when suddenly I found myself surrounded by a large pack of dogs, all looking identical and being led on identical corretges by identical masters. I had barely looked at them when the dogs turned into ocelots, so that I was now faced with a large group of identical ocelots on identical corretges held by identical masters. And before I could think the ocelots turned into people, identical people on identical corretges held by... different masters this time, who were all gats—gats of different sizes and colors, a splendid speckled swarm of gats!

More than once I marveled, astonished, at people's ability and desire to spend such extensive amounts of time indoors, among ridiculous paraphernalia and ridiculous beings, as opposed to exploring the magic of the outdoors, of trees and birds and happy butterflies. Trees offer a much superior view upon the world to the one presented by finestres, for they stand in the immediate proximity of nature—in the very midst of it, in fact,—and thus allow one to observe and sniff and feel the world with much greater keenness. For my part, whenever I found myself in places which did not allow me to while away a goodly amount of time in trees, as is the custom of ocelots, I grew not only irritated, but also sickly, with a much decreased appetite for both life and food. I couldn't tell you whether I felt weak because I ate little or ate little because I felt weak, but lack of nourishment and lack of vigor seemed always to mingle and cause me trouble. If somehow I caught a glimpse of myself in a mirall at such times, I couldn't help but feel sorry for the pitiful figure that met my eyes. At the same time, I found myself sleeping more at night than I usually did, worn out as I was by the daytime activities and the dearth of daytime naps. At such times I felt great shame at my perceived failure to hang onto my ocelot nature and my apparent surrender to the ways of people.

One time a great party of people assembled in that place from which Mar and I watched the jardin des tuileries, or the trees. The people arrived in waves upon waves, roughly five at a time, some of them in ridiculous entanglement of limbs, and settled into small chattering groups about the place. Mar and I quit the spot we had been dozing in, which was one of the spaces we favored, and moved quickly to an idle, still-quiet corner. The squealing crowd continued to disperse throughout the apartment, and at some point música came on the sound machine. As the noise grew louder and people came to occupy our new space, Mar and I became increasingly distraught. I stood up and started treading the place while looking for a new spot to settle in. I instructed Mar to follow me; she did so for a little while, then decided to stay put, taking refuge under a chance object. She was tired, she said. I nodded understandingly and continued to make my way through the multitude; soon I reached the apartment's porta, which was standing wide open and was looking beautiful for the first time. Feeling a rush of excitement, I surged forward into the great corridor which I had seen multiple times before and was thus familiar with. "Maybe this is it, freedom at last," I thought happily as I dashed toward the stairs. I was smiling inwardly and making plans as I started to descend. "Where to go, what to eat..." You can doubtless imagine my thoughts if you ever have been in a similar situation, on the verge of gaining much-craved freedom in a strange land. I was thus daydreaming when I felt the grip of a rough hand on my neck. Right away the hair on my back stood up in bristles. Peter had come for me, and in the firm clutches of his arms I felt renewed desperation, as if I had been cast into the deepest pit. I moped about for the remainder of the day, not knowing what to do with myself and wishing for the great crowd to be off, so that some relief could return to my glum existence. I was well tired of being pulled, pushed and prodded by repugnant hands, and wanted to get away from all things and all people—everything, in fact, apart from Mar. Now I had just failed, and what if another chance would never come again? What if the porta would remain forever closed? What would become of Mar and me? And how about my duty to other ocelots, the one I had once been so certain of being entrusted with? I secretly wept to see how hapless I was, how utterly powerless to vary even by a small degree the course of my life... A majestic ocelot reduced to a weakling!

Dream no. 37: I found myself in one of the fantastical machines transporting people and running on water. I felt so unutterably dizzy and sick, and so close to retching, that I decided to jump into the water, come what may. This I did, and as soon as I completed the jump I felt my body enveloped in a strange, soothing warmth. I resolved never to swim out, but to remain there forever, among the fish, like a prank played on them.

Sometime after the Perpignan affair, I noticed that Dalí was again laboring passionately on an image. This new project consumed much of his time, and during the undertaking Dalí often articulated—in conversation with himself and others—the words *homenatge, homenaje, hommage, pesca, tonyina, atún, meissonier*, and *géricault*. Indeed, he spoke those words with such frequency that it was as though an obsession had taken hold of him. Gala, Peter, Isidor, and even visitors all had to listen to Dalí's nattering about *pesca, atún,* and *géricault*. Dalí also made much reference to *todo el mundo* during his speeches, which Dos Pasos translated as being the entire world. I didn't know whether the wonderland was about the entire world, or about to be seen by the entire world, or something altogether different, but I felt caught up in Dalí's enthusiasm—as I had felt in the past,—and while it was possible I evaded the frustrations of my life by basking in the warmth of that feeling.

What awaited us at the conclusion of our trip on water was an environment much akin to the jardin des tuileries place. It was, in other words, yet another site of vast swarms of people and substantial raucousness. I had to endure a considerable number of inconveniences, but three things stand out as having been particularly irksome: the cotxes, the cold, and the people. The cotxes were hard-to-count and ear-splitting, as well as impossible to avoid by those venturing outside. The cold was extreme, making my body rise up in a shivering and shuddering protest. Occasionally white fluffy things would float down from above, stopping to rest in my fur and on the ground, and then I felt wonder and puzzlement in addition to annoyance at the chill gripping my body. The white fluffy things would even stay around for a while, covering the ground like a skin. (Gala derived much pleasure from the bitter cold and the fluffy things, she giggled with undeniable delight, which was further proof that people and ocelots have significantly different tastes.) As for the people, here too Dalí gathered crowds around him, forcing Mar and me to exist in their midst. Andy, Alfred, Bob, Frank, Lucille, and Sammy were some of the names which I thought I made out from among the multitudes. Andy seemed the most common presence, as well as a forbidding figure: I assisted, unwillingly and fearfully, at many conversations between him and Dalí.

I couldn't help thinking, looking at the roaming life of Dalí and his cohorts, that people bore some resemblance to a troop of stray gats: while they had homes and no apparent need to hunt or beg, as well as no observable master, people meandered from place to place in much the same way as the homeless gats whom I knew and called friends—though it seemed to me that people covered larger distances. As for those who crowded around Dalí, they did this in the same way that the vagrant, rough-living gats gathered around Dos Pasos, with manifest excitement and interest. I wondered then whether those people were downright tramps and whether Dalí could have been, in their eyes, as clever as Dos Pasos was in the world of gats.

In that bitterly cold place I beheld some ruc-like creatures who held my attention for a long time, both through their resemblance to the ruc and through their attachment to extraordinary contrivances which were apparently used, like the machines I had experienced, for the transport of people. I gazed and marveled, and would have gazed and marveled much longer had I not been dragged away by Peter, who was then controlling my corretja. One time I actually witnessed Dalí and Gala get onto one of those contrivances and become carried off by one of the ruc-like beasts; I watched them with a sort of pining until they disappeared from my sight.

At times great bodies of water came down upon us, reminding me of times from the past when I had listened to them swish through the trees. On a number of occasions they had been accompanied by fantastic, frightful booms and the emergence of immense lights far above whose life had seemed a mere moment. I had felt intensely scared in such instants, and had unfailingly rushed to my mother and pressed my body against hers, trying to gain at least partial cover from the pelting beast. My mother had explained that this was a periodic phenomenon which simply had to be waited out. Once it passed, nothing remained apart from general dampness and freshened air, and it was easy to wonder whatever had caused my terror. Without my mother, however, I was easy prey for the beast and the horror it inflicted upon my being: all I could do was attempt to crouch down within myself and to ignore the rumblings of my heart. The people seemed to possess a kind of remedy for such times: they covered their bodies with intricate and colorful objects which lent them a ridiculous air but were meant, by all appearances, to protect them from the menace. The people did not display, on these occasions, any more agitation than was typical of them, so I concluded that they did not feel the fear that I felt.

As my new life carried on, and I met ever more people and attended ever more events—through sheer coercion rather than my own desires—the ability to remember my dreams diminished. I still counted them, which in itself felt like a formidable task, but found it harder and harder to access their substance. I can see three main reasons for this, although one could say that they are all reducible to one thing: the nature of my existence. First, the countless things which I had to keep learning and the numerous people whom I kept encountering caused me to live in a state of perpetual anxiety, tension, exasperation, and weariness. Secondly, the awful racket which engulfed me at most times had a hurtful influence on the workings of my mind, and on my capacity to remain calm and relaxed—as ocelots always are in the land, when not in danger or in the hunting process. Thirdly, the fact that people decided the whats, whos, wheres, and hows of my life meant that I could not slumber and awaken when and as I wished: a nap being cut short could mean that a dream was interrupted, or that I didn't have sufficient time, post-snooze, to process a dream. For these disconcerting reasons, I can only recount to you the dreams which my mind succeeded in retaining.

After some time passed in my new life, a time which

seemed long and suffered with much inner torment and physical struggle, I received the terrible news that Fiord perished, having been hit by a cotxe. Aigua and Dos Pasos were visibly downcast, all the more so since they hadn't seen the accident happen and hadn't been able to come to Fiord's rescue. They simply found him lying on the ground, breathless and cold. They thought it must have been a cotxe, that's what it usually was, and in our area cotxes were sparse but even more dangerous for that reason: a cotxe could appear out of nowhere and strike an un-cautious or too-innocent gat. We thought of gentle Fiord, with his easy-going nature, silky voice, soft fur, and felt unspeakably forlorn at his disappearance. A short time later another gat came along, one who'd always been a vagabond and apparently wandered in from a nearby area. Aigua and Dos Pasos befriended him and named him Spritz—this being a word which Dos Pasos had heard during his time with Dolors and which he'd never forgotten. Spritz knew more about cotxes than Fiord had, so Aigua and Dos Pasos hoped that he would be around longer, to keep them company. Spritz was a good fellow, kind and brave and mischievous: he jumped on the backs of his new playmates whenever he thought he wouldn't incur their wrath. So now there were three gats again. Mar and I joined them at night and sometimes during the day, and every now and again we thought of Fiord and pictured him sprinting toward us.

Around the time that Spritz arrived, Dalí began toiling away at a new wonderland, this one being about *corrida*, *venus*, *torero*, and *trompe l'oeil,* whatever those things were. This particular wonderland, seemingly no less important than the *perpignan* and the *atún* projects, induced more muttering than excited talk in Dalí. Mar and I were quite neglected during this time—and a long time it was,—apart from those occasions when we were dragged on trips. It bothered me that Dalí's inattention left me with little opportunity to learn, especially about his work, but at the same time I used the unencumbered time to sit alone with my musings and reveries, or play games with Mar and the gats.

Dream no. 48: In this briefest of all my dreams, Fiord appeared to me and said that he now had a master and a home, the best of masters and the best of homes, and he was happy.

My education was largely limited to my reveries, the dialogues with Mar and the gats, the matters which Dalí and others elucidated for me—in the rare moments which they devoted to this task—and the conclusions I drew from observing the talks, interactions, and behaviors of people. In the course of time, my ears caught references to all manner of things—things such as *dólares, pesetas, buckminster fuller, lorca, oda, llanto, chien andalou, buñuel, breton, nadja, fabre, picasso, millet, angelus, don juan, william tell, ventafocs, gowans, corrida, impresionista, cinco delatarde, cadaqués, sirenas, pescadores, davinci, franco, arp, aficionado, tristan undisolde, freud, miró, gaudí*—but I could only ever tease out the meanings of a paltry few. Moreover, enlightenment itself brought complications. For instance, I worked out that two words together represented people's names; it therefore followed that Buckminster Fuller, Chien Andalou, Don Juan, William Tell, Cinco Delatarde, and Tristan Undisolde were people. These were not individuals I had ever seen with Dalí, I realized upon mulling over their names, but given Dalí's inclination to spend much time in company, and the fact that these beings were frequently talked about, I felt certain that they would make an appearance sooner or later. This gave me something to do when people came to visit Dalí and when we went out for walks, as I watched for the emergence of Buckminster, Chien, Cinco, Tristan, and the others. Yet for all my watchfulness these people never showed up, never came to either entertain or be entertained. This forced me to revisit my theory, which I decided to do by consulting Dos Pasos. (Mar's conjectures were as confusing as my own.) That wisest of gats was entirely unaware of Buckminster Fuller, William Tell, or Tristan Undisolde. He did, however, know something about Chien Andalou, Don Juan, and Cinco Delatarde. Chien was another word for dog, that dreadful creature who was all too happy to be carried around on a corretja, while Andalou must have been—Dos Pasos guessed,—a dog's name. Don Juan was a hero in a llibre, like the ruc. Cinco Delatarde was not a human, but rather an expression somehow related to people's comings and goings. I felt greatly disheartened by both Dos Pasos' ignorance and my own. Moreover, it weighed on me that I had imagined Chien Andalou to be a person who had a dog named Buñuel, though I had never shared this with anyone. Now if Chien himself was a dog, it followed that he was the one most likely owned! For some reason, the thought bothered me: having my ideas contradicted by reality—for I took it that Dos Pasos was right—was a most unpleasant experience. I seemed to register even less success with individual words and expressions than I did with names, or presumed names. While I could see that certain relationships existed, and that *lorca, oda,* and *llanto* were somehow related, and so were *cadaqués, sirenas,* and *pescadores,* I could never tell the meaning of either the words or their relationships.

Notwithstanding the general disregard shown to Mar and me, there were two instances when I had the chance to directly observe Dalí at work (or play), and when some explanation was provided. The first such instance was an outing with Dalí to the playa, sometime after Dalí's *atún* project and before his *corrida* undertaking. Mar stayed behind on that particular occasion, for reasons which I do not recall. I was bored and somewhat drowsy, as I often was during the day. At the beach we encountered a man who kindly gave me several fish to eat; that boosted my spirits a little. After talking to the man, Dalí fiddled with some objects of the sort I had glimpsed in the forbidden room, tethered me to a boulder, and proceeded to engage in yet more fiddling—while the creature just encountered sat down before us, toying with the thing out of which he had taken the fish. Soon Dalí put up a flat object between himself and the beast, which caused me to guess that he was preparing to do the very things he did in the forbidden room. And so it was! Dalí became wholly absorbed in his activity, his eyes moving quickly between the man and the object I just mentioned. As I stood watching, my mouth nearly agape with wonder and incredulity, this object kept changing its appearance, and by the time we left the playa—quite some time later, I fancied—I could tell that it had started to resemble the scene before Dalí. This was my first time witnessing the evolution of Dalí's work, and I couldn't wait to share my excitement with Mar.

The second instance I directly witnessed Dalí's work occurred, I believe, right during the time when Dalí was laboring on his *corrida* project. One day Dalí invited Mar and me inside the forbidden room, with Peter holding us on corretges, and tried—as we assumed—to explain what he was doing. He pointed to the image before him, which revealed something that looked like a tree with some creatures at its top and its bottom, and then pointed to other images lying about the room. He spoke all the while, loudly and firmly, in a tone which nearly frightened me. I strived to keep my concentration, however, for I liked the images and felt that I had finally been invited to a true learning session. While there was much that I could not make sense of, I noticed that Dalí repeated the words *cuadro, alice*, and *wonderland*. I couldn't tell what was what, but guessed that *wonderland* might be Dalí's word for image, people's designation for the thrilling objects found in that room. When the lesson was over, which happened in too short a while, I asked Mar for her opinion. Like me, Mar didn't know what was what; we therefore agreed that *wonderlands* would henceforth be the name of the images which Dalí made, and *wonderland-maker* would be our name for Dalí.

Shortly after the learning session in Dalí's forbidden room I had dream no. 56: I was walking with Dalí and Peter, or rather being walked, around one of the disorienting places I was often taken to during trips. I was on the point of being led into yet another one of the enclosures which people call stores or boutiques or tiendas when I decided to break free and run away. I jerked my head in all directions, strained at the corretja, and used all the force of my body to pull away from the two men leading me. After a brief, tough battle I escaped. I dashed off without looking back, tearing at a few objects which lay annoyingly in my path. I came to a halt before a girl who immediately started addressing me: "Hello, Eli. My name is Alice." Before I could work out why it was that I understood her language, or why it was that she knew my name, she said, "I will take you back; let's go." As soon as she'd finished speaking I found myself back in the land, Alice having disappeared and my mother having appeared in her place. I rushed to embrace mamma, and we proceeded to playfully tackle each other.

Gala began to show herself less and less around Dalí's place, and at some point Mar and I stopped seeing her altogether. (Gala re-emerged on some of the trips, but I felt nothing at her sight.) Yet Mar and I heard Dalí say her names in her absence, and guessed that—like ocelots,—people too thought and spoke of others who weren't around anymore. (There was no telling whether Dalí and Gala had been brought together by the force of circumstance, which had driven Mar and me together, or by a different kind of force.) I thought of Gala's many names and concluded that they were a needless burden, for one had to keep in mind all the ways in which one could be called, one day Gradiva and another day Lionette. I then felt a new pride surge in me at the thought of my own name, which was now used solely by Mar and the gats. Eli. I wanted to hear my mother call me, which I imagined she must be doing. On some days I waited, straining my ears, on the off chance that I might hear her call. I never did.

One time I summoned up the courage to ask Mar about her own mother, and whether she had been wrenched from her in the same way that I was. Mar only growled unhappily in response, letting me know that she didn't wish to speak of the matter.

Dalí engaged in a great number of aggravating practices, something which led, over time, to the disillusionment of which I spoke earlier. To give you but one example: there were two pools of water near Dalí's house, a small one and a big one, and at times Dalí would throw me into the small one, watching to see my reaction. On each such occasion I swam out quickly while shooting Dalí a furious glance, for I did not enjoy the experience and moreover felt annoyed by Dalí's brazen ignorance of the well-known fact that while ocelots can swim, they only enter water when the catching of prey absolutely requires it. There was no prey there, nothing to catch, so the affair was merely a distasteful joke at my expense. "What a fool," I would think to myself, for what sort of being could be so uninformed and moreover so deriving of pleasure from others' visible distress? I had no doubt, in light of these and other incidents, that Dalí was indeed a fool—or else a being in a perpetual state of *faire le clown.* There were, in the final analysis, only three things which I liked about Dalí: his images, or *wonderlands*, as Mar and I decided to call them; the rare moments when Dalí took time to explain things to Mar and me, in what we took to be a poor attempt to educate us; and the times when Dalí sat outside dozing, much as we ocelots did.

Dream no. 60: Here Mar and I decided to attack Dalí in his sleep, in revenge for the wretched expeditions and petty pranks forced upon our delicate, sensitive bodies. Mar appeared more eager and animated than I had ever seen her, chuckling happily and striding determinedly beside me. I gobbled up all of Dalí's mitjons before setting off, with Mar, to look for our pitiless master. We found him asleep in the forbidden room, a big wonderland upon his chest. We watched the slumbering figure for a while, and saw its moustache twitch. Mar and I couldn't decide whether to merely hurt or to kill Dalí, and how to go about it. The wonderland seemed to stand in the way of our plan, half-considered as it was. We looked more closely at the image, and noticed that it was comprised of all the things and people that inhabited our life. Even Mar and I made an appearance, in one of the wonderland's corners. We became so absorbed in analyzing the image, with all its fanciful elements, that we entirely forgot about taking revenge upon Dalí.

While Dalí made wonderlands of many things, he never made one of Mar or myself. Why he didn't, I couldn't tell you: ocelots are quite obviously marvelous creatures with handsome features, who would make exquisite pictures! Mar suggested that having an image made of oneself might require one to remain motionless for long stretches of time—so it seemed, based on our observations of Dalí's work,— and might therefore be rather inconvenient for us, unless Dalí was happy to capture us napping in various corners. If Mar was right, then it was fortunate that Dalí never showed a desire to make images of us; the inert butterflies in his house, who never complained of their condition, seemed much better suited to the role of targets for image-making. Given this state of affairs, I was greatly surprised one day when Dalí brought out an image of the two of us, meaning him and myself, and pointing emphatically to it hollered, "Eres famoso, Babou! Eres famoso!" I didn't know what Dalí's fuss meant and didn't much care, for I became intensely absorbed by the inexplicable image. Soon afterward I went to consult Dos Pasos, as I often did when confounded by mysteries. He didn't know how the image could have materialized, but said that *famoso* was a word associated with the heroes found in llibres, heroes like the ruc, so I might be one of them. Dos Pasos believed that those heroes were distinguished in some way, and well-liked; he then added, softly and sadly, that he'd never seen any image of himself. I took some time to think over these findings. I failed to see any resemblance between me and llibre heroes: my exploits did not strike me as exceptional, and I was not distinguished in any way except perhaps through my suffering. Nevertheless, if I came to be known by any means whatsoever, then there was a chance that my mother would hear of me. And if I never managed to become renowned through being a learned ocelot, as I had once dreamed, then being known for nothing in particular might just serve my purpose. At the same time, it occurred to me that no one, among all the creatures I had come to know, was more deserving of the hero title than Dos Pasos: his wisdom—if not knowledge—was unsurpassed in the world of animals, no doubt outdoing that of humans in any fair tussle of minds. The thought that Dos Pasos was not famoso, and his wonderfulness not truly recognized, made me feel quite revolted and caused me to forget, for a while, about my life's asperities.

Dream no. 64: I found myself inside Dalí's forbidden room, contemplating a wonderland which I knew he had recently made. To my astonishment, the image stared back at me, with the very eyes that I stared at it. I jumped when I recognized the resemblance, indeed the perfect likeness, after which I started pacing about and growling. I wanted the image to talk to me, so I tried to provoke it. I said that we should connect, make friends, perhaps teach each other a thing or two. The image remained silent, so I gave it a poke to prove that I only sought its friendship, that no harm was intended. There was no response, so I tapped on one of its ears. There was still no reaction, so I tapped on its nose. I waited a while, but only silence came. I became sad, then offended, then angry. The image was still watching me, with eyes which made me realize that it was refusing my friendship on purpose, that enmity was its intention. I watched it a while longer, to confirm my suspicions, then launched my assault upon it. The image did not strike back, which felt like another insult, so I continued to unleash my anger. I hit it until I knocked it over, until it collapsed with a thud before my feverish being. Now it was gone, and I was all alone, no eyes upon me.

No matter how admirable Dalí's wonderlands might have been, I had not the slightest doubt that I could produce images of comparable, even surpassing, value. I would never reproduce what was right in front of my eyes, with an exception made for Mar and mamma, but rather I would depict my strange many-colored dreams, with their extravagant beings and events. That I never had the chance to show my abilities, to prove myself in this way and others, to reveal the wondrous world within my soul and my dreams, I can only deem a profound misfortune, a catastrophe of the first order.

Partir, c'est mourir un peu, someone said, I don't know who, and it took me a long time to decipher the meaning of this saying, but I did, it means to leave is to die a little, and indeed this was what leaving always meant for me, dying a little. Each journey left me feeling more strained and glum, more jittery and troubled. Those trips of a protracted sort ended up, over time, causing me to regard my life as a long series of rooms, or else one vast dismal room which forever thwarted my attempts to live a natural, ocelot life. Periodically I was made to return to Dalí's house, and remained there until the next trip occurred; I returned to that place as to a home, even though it wasn't a home, and nowhere else was home.

The memory of my time with mamma, once rich and vibrant, filled with sights and smells and sensations, gradually faded into a kind of muted música, a slight murmur, the intimation of a bolting beast. Mamma's very face began to elude me, and the more I called the more it fled, the more I sought the more it slipped. I yearned to exist once more in its shadow, to follow its lead, to watch it as I watched the drom and its subtle movements, to be lulled to sleep by its restful eyes. I believe that the last time I saw her was in dream no. 71: It was night-time and I was outside, gazing at the drom and the schlundewassens. As I was admiring them, the drom quickly turned into a rabbit, who then turned into a tree, which then turned into a monkey, who then turned into my mother. I couldn't touch her and she couldn't touch me; she was close by and far away; I could only see and hear. Mamma looked sad, and sadly she spoke to me. She said that the land was no longer the way I had known it: the shrubbery and the animals were disappearing, and ocelots could not live there much longer. She then beseeched me not to return, repeating her message several times. "Do not come back, Eli, do not come back, do not come back."

Upon returning from one of my long tiresome unwanted trips I was informed by Aigua that Dos Pasos had vanished: one day he'd failed to turn up at their customary meeting, and proved to be nowhere to be found. (This happened, according to Aigua, a short while after a prodigious vent blew through the area, a vent of a type which always came during the times I was gone.) Aigua and Spritz—for this happened sometime after Fiord's dreadful death by cotxe— searched desperately for Dos Pasos, penetrated all the nooks and crannies they could think of, asked gats from farther regions if they'd spotted him, all to no avail. Needless to say, this was a devastating blow to the spirits of all who were friends of the wise old gat. There is no way to properly describe how much we owed Dos Pasos, how much we had depended on him, and how dear and precious he was to us.

Shortly after the news about Dos Pasos' disappearance, I noticed a change in Mar: she became more quiet and withdrawn, her body seemingly overcome by torpor and her eyes taken over by hollowness. Now, it is a fact well-known to ocelots, though possibly not to people, that silence can be louder than the loudest of noises, more telling of the sorrows or joys of the beings upholding it; indeed, this is why I have always been a friend of silence, and silence a friend of mine. This being so, I thought that I perceived, in Mar's new way of being, the story of a numbness, a dissolution of strength and will, a mournful wasting away. I didn't quite know how to offer solace, especially on those occasions when I myself felt disconsolate, so I often ended up simply keeping Mar unobtrusive company. It looked to me as though she and I were, in this new phase—one of no games and no pleasures, outside the time spent with Aigua and Spritz—companionable lonelinesses brushing past each other, every so often bumping heads through sheer accident.

I liked Mar.
I hope she liked me.
I hope she could tell I liked her.
I never told her anything about this.
I never learned any good words for this purpose.

I discerned in time that certain expressions kept turning up in Dalí's speech; they were repeated on multiple occasions, sometimes in the course of the same day. I wish I could tell you their meaning, but each and every one of them was accompanied by a variety of wild gestures which pointed to nothing specific—not to mention that they were spoken in the midst of agitated conversations with assorted people,—and this greatly hindered my ability to reach a definitive conclusion. In any case, these are the phrases which I made out and can recall:

El peixos grossos sempre es menjaran els minuts.

Prometre no fa povre.

L'àliga no caça mosques.

Obra començada, mig acabada.

No hi ha gloria sense enveja.

La pela es la pela.

Ratolí que no més coneix un forat, està atrapat.

If one were to undertake a rigorous analysis of my studies, I imagine that one would inevitably come to the conclusion that despite my considerable efforts to become a learned ocelot, and despite my partial success in doing so, I failed in innumerable ways, and perhaps was doomed to remain forever far from the goal of being cultivé and renowned. I have made my peace with this judgment, and have moreover realized that of all the existent and feasible methods of learning, none was ever more pleasurable to me than my daydreams. While they do not contain many precise answers, daydreams make for a more vivid and boundless space than life does: everything is possible within one's fanciful thoughts, where I could even talk to the drom and the schlundewassens, but not so within the edges of one's routine existence. This is why, even while trying to learn in all other ways, I was always happy to return to solitude and reverie, to peace and contemplation.

I often thought, in the course of my reveries, that a different master—if I had to accept one—would have been a vastly better match for me than Dalí and his companions: indeed, we might even have gotten along nicely. I liked to picture someone like Dolors for my master, or even the man that Dalí and I encountered at the playa: that man had a gentle air about him, an air very different from Dalí's, and I imagined him being good to me. I felt a pang of regret at my failure to ask that man to be my master right on the day we met, when he offered me the fish. Of course, there is no telling whether he could ever have managed to extricate me from my situation, or even whether he would have understood my plea. Still: I would never know, because I didn't ask. These reflections caused me to wonder whether people were any better than ocelots at unpuzzling the many mysteries of life—and if they were, were they filled with more peace and contentment than us ocelots? Were they less anguished and burdened? Less ashamed of their failures and shortcomings? I imagined that if I had the answers to all my queries, I would enjoy a liberation from the need to wonder, though I might be saddened by some of the answers.

Dream no. 77: I found myself suspended in non-space, faced with a creature whom I knew to be neither gat nor ocelot but still a member of the same enchanting family. This creature was a magnificent specimen, her dappled look not much different from an ocelot's, but she had a vaguely mournful air about her: a heaviness in her movement and a drooping in her head. She explained sadly, keeping her head low, that she had been driven away from her land, along with many others. I immediately had a vision of the others, a great mass of fine fellows—of different looks but like colors—who had been chased away. They all turned their eyes toward me. "You'll have to join us," said one. "You have no choice," added another. A chill ran down my back as they spoke, carrying with it an increasing fretfulness. Luckily, the dream ended at that instant.

In time, all my human companions mingled—in their fundamental sameness—into one body, the body of a creature alien and hostile to ocelots, a creature who should itself be put on a corretja if that could stop its limbs from grasping at things it isn't meant to possess. In time too, I started to have trouble distinguishing my life's events from the experiences of my dreams. Everything seemed real and unreal at the same time, and everything was bad too, nothing good was happening in either life or dreams. Indeed, I began to prefer—above all else—profound, uninterrupted slumber.

A time came, not long after the vanishing of Dos Pasos, when my mental and physical decline became inescapable, like a needy youngster trailing behind his parent and occasionally yelping for help. My former agility and quickness were gone, my limbs lacked their usual self-assurance, and my appetite for food and everything else was on a continual wane. I understood then, with hitherto never experienced clarity, my fundamental condition. All creatures are made to exist in a particular environment, one with meticulously chosen parameters—though I couldn't say who chooses those parameters—which satisfy the creatures' needs. Once snatched out of their natural climate, the beasts perish under the burden of physical or mental degradation, perhaps both; only the duration of this pitiful process varies from one being to another. A fish removed from his water element starts immediately to gasp for life, to thrash about in visible distress, and in only a little while, in the time required for him to be truly seen and understood, his life dissolves into the jaws or hands of his hunter. And the hunter? He too, if pulled away from his native surroundings, if alienated from the stamping grounds he calls home and which he longs to go back to, becomes tormented and diseased, and eventually succumbs to his assorted incurable ailments. I myself had been stamped out, squashed, destroyed, much like the fish—the only difference being that the dying process was more prolonged and tortuous in my case. And perchance this was the way of the world, perhaps I had no right to complain, possibly no injustice was ever committed and there was none to chide or ask reparations of. I now had the firm knowledge that I would never return to the land; even if some way I did, I was no longer able to hunt, and therefore would still find myself condemned to a slow and shameful death. Yes, I was no longer a hunter: a thought which had occasionally tried to burrow into my mind, but which I had stubbornly chased away each time, resolved as I had been to make an escape and go back to the land from which I'd come.

I began to retreat more and more from all manner of activities, indeed from the entire routine of life, excusing myself briefly and hiding in various nooks and corners to escape involvement and ballyhoo. To my intense surprise, Dalí and his cohorts began—for the first time—to respect my wishes and leave me to my own devices. So I would sit alone for long stretches of time, gazing with new and intrigued eyes upon the world around me. Now and then I beheld a sight, often that of a plain insect or bird dancing about in the daytime air, which filled my heart with pure joy. Little by little I started to experience a new kind of freedom, one never known before, which seemed to be born out of an inkling of having eluded the humans who made me live among them, of not having belonged to them after all. I was going to slip away, perhaps not in the way I had envisioned for so long, but slip away all the same. One of these days my anguished mind, set free, would command my worn-out limbs to go, and one foot after another would obey, and I'd be gone.